"I dedicate this book to my family, friends, and colleagues whose unwavering support and great advice made this book better than I could have by myself." ~ Mark "Dr. D" Damohn

"To my wife Helene and our children whose patience, support, and inspiration have made my creative career possible." ~ Gene Hotaling

ISBN: 1-932888-65-9

Printed in the United States.

# T'WAS THE NIGHT BEFORE KICKOFF

GO GATORS!

Written By
Mark "Dr. D" Damohn

Illustrations By
Gene Hotaling

T'was the night before kickoff

And all through the Swamp

All the Gators were ready,

Ready to stomp.

Florida Field was
Manicured with care

Knowing that another
Victim would soon be there.

This is the kind of fun
With other Gators  Albert and
Alberta like To share.

The visitors don't want to be there
'Cause the Gators will
Put them Into quite a scare.

Albert and Alberta were snug in
Their beds with that Gator Grin
Stitched on their heads.

They know that it fills their foes
With so much dread.

Alberta in her nightgown
And Albert with his Gator cap
Had just settled down for a nice
Pre-Victory nap.

When out on the field

There arose such a squeal.

The Gators were chompin'

Ready for another meal.

Away to the pressbox window
Albert flew like a flash.

He's not going to miss tomorrow

Knowing the Gators are going
To have a really big bash.

The moon was full and
Gave a very nice glow

To the freshly cut
Field far below.

Albert smiled about the
Victory he would know.

As Albert was watching the
The pageant unfold

Memories of victories came
Flooding back from days of old.

The Gators shucked the Bucks
41 to 14.

Oh the memories, so very sweet.

A couple of years after it was to be

Florida 24 and Oklahoma 14.

It was another great Gator victory

For another great Gator team

Because

Sooner or later

If you're not a Gator

You will be Gator Bait !!!!

But the memory that made Albert
Grin from Gator ear to Gator ear

Was 1996, Oh what a year.

The Gators ran the SEC
For many a year

But went to Tally
And got a late hit.

Then to Atlanta and rolled
Back the Tide every little bit.

Then onto the Big Easy and
Re-met those Tally Noles.

There was a score to settle
From that punch in the nose.

In the end it was 52 to 20.

Revenge was sweet.

Revenge was plenty.

But that was then
And this is now

The opponents are going to let
Out a really big yowl.

The Gators go into the
Swamp and on to the field

Arrives the Orange and
Blue Men of Steel.

The opponents all they can
Do is tremble and shake

'Cause the Gators are about to
Show some Shake and Bake.

The Gators can pass
Or they can run.

Our boys are having
So much fun.

The Gators score points galore.

We love it. We want more.

The Gators will have their way

From our smothering defense

To our blistering offense

They can't get away

No matter what they say.

The Gators are so intense.

We rule the day.

With ball in hand
The Gators will go.

Leaving all the others
To simply say whoa.

The opponents Leave the
Field with heads hung low

Because they have just been
Hit and run over by
A big Swamp Gator Floe.

But on they came - Volunteers,
Wildcats, Rebels, and Tides

Hang on tight.
It's going to be a bumpy ride.

On came Tigers, Gamecocks,
Hogs and Vandy.

We'll all be excited.
The game should be a dandy.

Also arrived Bulldogs, Tally
Noles, and even a Hurricane.

But remember this is our house.
The Gators shall reign!!!

These Gators are brothers,
Such a band

The bond is strong,
The strongest in the land.

The Gators are tough
And in command.

So the foes surrender
And throw up their hands.

The opponents were so badly beat.

They could not get on their feet.

They were at Ben Hill
And could not survive.

'Cause in the Swamp
Only Gators get out alive.

So by the end of the game

The results are still the same.

Another Gator conquest.

Which always shows the rest

That the Gators are still the best.

The Gators are at the top.
There is no room

The Gators had lowered the boom.
Forcing the foes to
leave the Swamp

In their Orange and very
Blue state of gloom.

But Albert and Alberta
Are alive with glee.

High Fiving Gator fans
Like you and me.

Along with Mr. Two-Bits
They start the Wave

To celebrate the victory to
us fans they gave.

As Albert leads the
Gators in cheer

For Gator fans far
And Gator fans near

Alberta looks so cute in her
Orange and Blue bow

But this is something all
Gator fans already know.

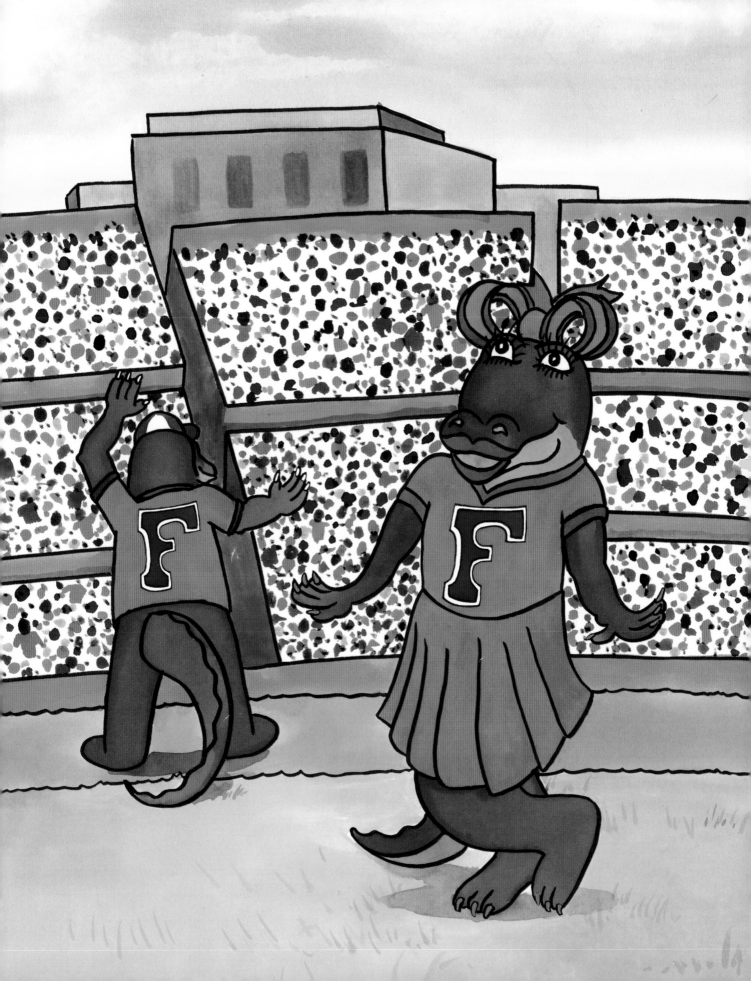

With another Gator
Victory in hand

The SEC is the Gators
To command.

The Gators know they
Are the very best

And there are simply the rest.

As Albert and Alberta left the field

They left to thunderous appeal

Knowing in their hearts

All others would have to yield.